Prologue

Near Tromso, Norway, St. Nicholas and the entire Elvish team have made their home for many, many years. Every Elvish youth, anywhere in the world, may spend a few years as an apprentice there. There, they learn from experts in any of the fields supporting St. Nicholas' mission to bring hope, joy, and presents to all the world's children.

Of all the Elves, the kindest, wisest and most senior is Raspinel. Old friends, he and St. Nicholas have always run this global enterprise together.

Love and kindness have no season. All year long, St. Nicholas and his whole team show this toward all living things. No task is too small, and no life is unimportant.

During a walk through the woods one Spring morning, St. Nick and Raspinel came upon a pair of strange, jewel-like eggs beside a fallen tree. The hatchlings became a source of amazement and entertainment for the two old friends' households and their community.

Raspinel   ras PIN' el
Zoe   ZO' ee

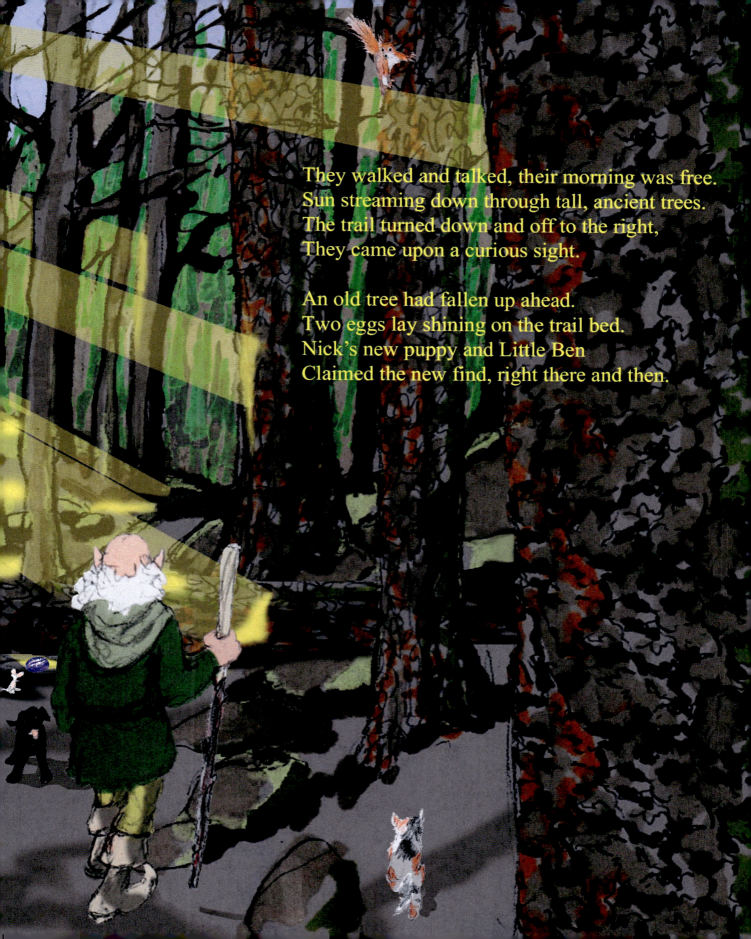

They walked and talked, their morning was free.
Sun streaming down through tall, ancient trees.
The trail turned down and off to the right,
They came upon a curious sight.

An old tree had fallen up ahead.
Two eggs lay shining on the trail bed.
Nick's new puppy and Little Ben
Claimed the new find, right there and then.

"These eggs are strange," Raspinel said.
"Quite new to me." He scratched his head.

Warmed by a dragon, guarded by a wolf,
About time to hatch, 'neath Raspinel's roof.

"How's the puppy?" "She seems ok,
She's gaining weight now, ev'ry day."
"What kind is she?" "It's not quite fixed,
She's partly Lab, but, surely mixed."

"Has Zoe named her yet?" "It's tricky,
As you know, I'm not too picky,
But, it's strange, she calls her 'Nicky.'"

"This little owl is quite a sight!
His colors are so very bright!
I think his name can be Neon,
So, his brother..." "How 'bout Xenon?"

"Raspinel, I'm amazed they talk!"
"Sannick, we're not some dumb-dumb hawks!"
"But, you're so young, you've just been born!"
The owls just blinked, then glared with scorn.

Raspinel coughed. Nicholas frowned.
Hard to not laugh - these birds are clowns.
"Smart as the dickens, little owl!"
"What's a 'dickens,' my big white pal?"

Nick couldn't help it, he laughed out loud.
Xenon looked puzzled, but he felt proud.
Nick laughed until tears ran down his cheeks,
Head back, Xenon just peered down his beak.

"We have to help them learn to fly,
Or they'll just sit as days go by.
They'll need to slip between the trees
And learn to coast upon the breeze"

"They think we have to learn to fly,
Practice, practice, try and try.
I don't know why they think it so,
They want to help, we can't say no."

"Physics are simple, thrust, drag, lift,
And our light weight is quite a gift!"

"Come on! Let's race to that big tree!
We'll take off when I count to three!

"Your onion soup was oh, so good!
Round of applause, we really should.
Blackened salmon? Looks fantastic -
This is nothing short of magic!"

"Wolf is playing with the owls?"
"They're far too quick for him, he howls."

"Neon, with your feathers bright,
You're better than the best flashlight!
Would you light Nick's and Zoe's way?"
"Be glad to, Ras'nel. 'Tis child's play!"

"I'm bored! Let's have some fun today!
Xenon, don't let me hear you say,
'It's very far, I do say so,
We'll be too tired with miles to go!'"

"Adjust your wings, control your speed,
And then just glide - it's all you need!
You really want to feel alive?
Tuck in your wings and then you dive!"

"Whoa! That's a puppy in the road!
The car's too fast - it hasn't slowed!"
The owls, in horror hovered there,
Wings beating slowly in the air.

They looked - the car had passed on by,
It hadn't hit the little guy!
They shot like arrows to his side.
"We'd better give this dog a ride!"

You are so lucky, little one!
We thought for sure that you were done!
The car was too fast for this rain,
It's good to hear you bark again!

We'll take you home, and get you dry!
They'll feed you soon, now, there, don't cry!
You'll like it in our forest home -
And when you're good, you'll get a bone!

"We found him, Ras'nel, on the road.
A car just missed him, never slowed.
Here he is. (This weather's yucky.)
By the way, we named him Lucky!"

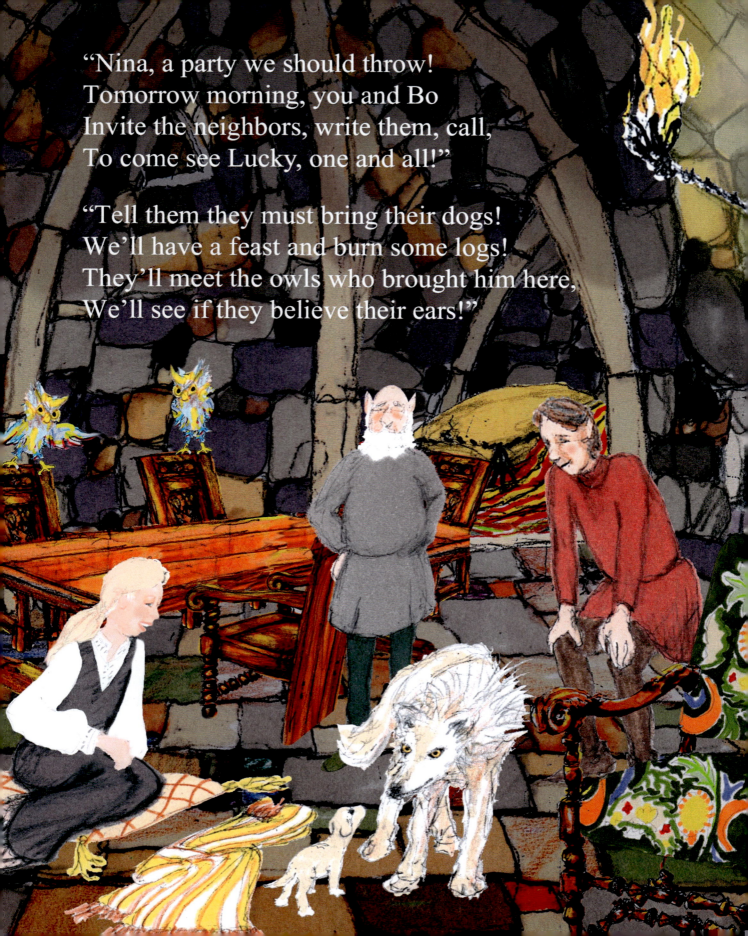

"Nina, a party we should throw!
Tomorrow morning, you and Bo
Invite the neighbors, write them, call,
To come see Lucky, one and all!"

"Tell them they must bring their dogs!
We'll have a feast and burn some logs!
They'll meet the owls who brought him here,
We'll see if they believe their ears!"

"Please come to picnic - Saturday.
And bring the dogs! They all can play!
Wolf now has a little brother,
A Lab pup without its mother."

Grown-ups, children, and dogs galore,
Most had been many times before.
The neighbors came from miles around,
Raspinel's place was friendly ground.

This didn't happen every week,
The parties were always unique.
The best of food and fellowship
And always more than worth the trip!

Lucky felt a wee little tug,
His first reaction, just a shrug.
Then Nicky bit a little more,
And that's how Lucky's ear was sore!

"That Lucky needs to learn to choose
From all his many puppy moves,
The ones that cats might deem okay
Instead of those that start a fray."

The sun is down, the torches low,
Their light a dimming, golden glow.

Neon, Xenon, Lucky and Wolf,
Bed down to sleep beneath their roof,
To dream of creeks, and romps, and flight,
At peace within the starry night.

Raspinel's House

Nicholai Fjord, Norway

The house is underground for warmth in winter, and Raspinel's preference for understatement.
One has to be very close to even see it.

He could have built anything, and this is what he chose.

Also by Russell Claxton

THE ST. NICHOLAS YORKIES
SAVING CHRISTMAS DAY

A Christmas tale of near-disaster, and a spirited response from the people and dogs of York.

The story will probably delight anyone who's ever known a dog.

Or a reindeer.

Or a cat.

ST. NICHOLAS AND FRIENDS
THE WHOLE YEAR ROUND

Come along for the ride! See how St. Nicholas and friends spend the year of 1947 having fun and getting ready for the long night's work on Christmas Eve.

ST. NICHOLAS IN PARIS
PRESIDENTS, POODLES, AND PARADES

1959. An invitation from the president of France brings St. Nick and the whole team to Paris for a visit, the Carnival, and a state dinner in appreciation for his work.

There were some surprises, too.

www.blueigloobooks.com

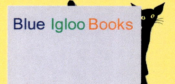

About the author

Russell Claxton, a Texas native, has called Macon, Georgia home for over twenty-five years with his wife Natalie and a string of dogs, cats and wildlife.

He is a practicing architect and urban designer. The conservation of natural resources runs high on his list of priorities.

Animal well-being is a life-long preoccupation, with accompanying enjoyment and appreciation of dogs, cats and lots of other animal friends.

Made in the USA
Columbia, SC
14 August 2022